CHILDREN'S THRIFT CLASSICS

Aladdin
and Other Favorite Arabian Nights Stories

EDITED BY PHILIP SMITH

Illustrated by Thea Kliros

D0376222

DOVER PUBLICATIONS, INC.
New York

DOVER CHILDREN'S THRIFT CLASSICS
EDITOR: PHILIP SMITH

Copyright © 1993 by Dover Publications, Inc.
All rights reserved under Pan American and International Copyright Conventions.

Published in Canada by General Publishing Company, Ltd., 30 Lesmill Road, Don Mills, Toronto, Ontario.

Aladdin and Other Favorite Arabian Nights Stories, first published by Dover Publications, Inc., in 1993, is a new anthology containing slightly corrected texts of six previously published English-language versions of Arabian Nights stories. "Aladdin and the Wonderful Lamp" is from Andrew Lang (ed.), *The Arabian Nights Entertainments* (Longmans, Green, and Co., London, 1898 [Dover reprint edition 0-486-22289-6]). The other five tales are from the anonymous publication *Stories from the Arabian Nights* (Charles E. Graham & Co., Newark, N.J. & New York, n.d.). The illustrations and introductory Note have been specially created for this edition.

Library of Congress Cataloging-in-Publication Data

Arabian nights. English. Selections. 1993.
Aladdin and other favorite Arabian nights stories / edited by Philip Smith ; illustrated by Thea Kliros.
p.   cm. — (Dover children's thrift classics)
Contents: Aladdin and the wonderful lamp — Abou Hassan, or, The sleeper awakened — Ali Baba and the forty thieves — The enchanted horse — Camaralzaman and Badoura — The seven voyages of Sindbad the sailor.
ISBN 0-486-27571-X (pbk.)
[1. Fairy tales. 2. Folklore, Arab.]   I. Smith, Philip, 1967–
II. Kliros, Thea, ill.   III. Series.
PZ8.A85   1993c
[398.22]—dc20   93–22073
                                                                CIP
                                                                AC

Manufactured in the United States of America
Dover Publications, Inc., 31 East 2nd Street, Mineola, N.Y. 11501

Note

The Arabian Nights, a large and diverse collection of popular stories, was gathered over a period of centuries from a multitude of Near Eastern countries. Its earliest portions are believed to be over 1000 years old; maintained through oral traditions and set down (and sometimes altered) by writers of many cultures, they represent a unique though often bewildering amalgam of folk traditions and literatures. The stories were introduced to the West in an early-eighteenth-century French translation, and have subsequently been retold and retranslated countless times. The *Arabian Nights* tales in this volume are among the most familiar to Western audiences, having been adapted into the popular media of the past three centuries: chapbooks, pantomimes, picture-books and live-action and animated motion pictures.

Contents

List of Illustrations

Aladdin and the Wonderful Lamp

THERE ONCE LIVED a poor tailor, who had a son called Aladdin, a careless, idle boy who would do nothing but play all day long in the streets with little idle boys like himself. This so grieved the father that he died; yet, in spite of his mother's tears and prayers, Aladdin did not mend his ways. One day, when he was playing in the streets as usual, a stranger asked him his age, and if he were not the son of Mustapha the tailor.

"I am, sir," replied Aladdin; "but he died a long while ago."

On this the stranger, who was a famous African magician, fell on his neck and kissed him, saying: "I am your uncle, and knew you from your likeness to my brother. Go to your mother and tell her I am coming."

Aladdin ran home, and told his mother of his newly found uncle.

"Indeed, child," she said, "your father had a brother, but I always thought he was dead."

However, she prepared supper, and bade Aladdin seek his uncle, who came laden with wine and fruit. He presently fell down and kissed the place where Mustapha used to sit, bidding Aladdin's mother not to be surprised at not having seen him before, as he had been forty years out of the country. He then turned to Aladdin, and asked him his trade, at which the boy hung his head, while his mother burst into tears. On learning that Aladdin was idle and would learn no trade, he offered to take a shop for him and stock it with merchandise. Next day he bought Aladdin a fine suit of clothes, and took him all over the city, showing him the sights, and brought him home at nightfall to his mother, who was overjoyed to see her son so fine.

Next day the magician led Aladdin into some beautiful gardens a long way outside the city gates. They sat down by a fountain, and the magician pulled a cake from his girdle, which he divided between them. They then journeyed onwards till they almost reached the mountains. Aladdin was so tired that he begged to go back, but the magician beguiled him with pleasant stories, and led him on in spite of himself.

At last they came to two mountains divided by a narrow valley.

"We will go no farther," said the false uncle. "I will show you something wonderful; only do you gather up sticks while I kindle a fire."

When it was lit the magician threw on it a powder he had about him, at the same time saying some magical words. The earth trembled a little and opened in front of them, disclosing a square flat stone with a brass ring in the middle to raise it by. Aladdin tried to run away, but the magician caught him and gave him a blow that knocked him down.

"What have I done, uncle?" he said piteously; whereupon the magician said more kindly: "Fear nothing, but obey me. Beneath this stone lies a treasure which is to be yours, and no one else may touch it, so you must do exactly as I tell you."

At the word treasure, Aladdin forgot his fears, and grasped the ring as he was told, saying the names of his father and grandfather. The stone came up quite easily and some steps appeared.

"Go down," said the magician; "at the foot of those steps you will find an open door leading into three large halls. Tuck up your gown and go through them without touching anything, or you will die instantly. These halls lead into a garden of fine fruit trees. Walk on till you come to a niche in a terrace where stands a lighted lamp. Pour out the oil it contains and bring it to me." He drew a ring from his finger and gave it to Aladdin, bidding him prosper.

Aladdin found everything as the magician had said, gathered some fruit off the trees, and, having got the lamp, arrived at the mouth of the cave. The magician cried out in a great hurry:

"Make haste and give me the lamp." This Aladdin refused to do until he was out of the cave. The magician flew into a terrible passion, and throwing some more powder on the fire, he said something, and the stone rolled back into its place.

The magician left the region at once, which plainly showed that he was no uncle of Aladdin's, but a cunning magician who had read in his magic books of a wonderful lamp, which would make him the most powerful man in the world. Though he alone knew where to find it, he could only receive it from the hand of another. He had picked out the foolish Aladdin for this purpose, intending to get the lamp and kill him afterwards.

For two days Aladdin remained in the dark, crying and lamenting. At last he clasped his hands in prayer, and in so doing rubbed the ring, which the magician had forgotten to take from him. Immediately an enormous and frightful genie rose out of the earth, saying:

"What wouldst thou with me? I am the Slave of the Ring, and will obey thee in all things."

Aladdin fearlessly replied: "Deliver me from this place!" whereupon the earth opened, and he found himself outside. As soon as his eyes could bear the light he went home, but fainted on the threshold. When he came to himself he told his mother what had passed, and showed her the lamp and the fruits he had gathered in the garden, which were in reality precious stones. He then asked for some food.

"Alas! child," she said, "I have nothing in the house, but I have spun a little cotton and will go and sell it."

Aladdin bade her keep her cotton, for he would sell the lamp instead. As it was very dirty she began to rub it, that it might fetch a higher price. Instantly a hideous genie appeared, and asked what she would have. She fainted away, but Aladdin, snatching the lamp, said boldly:

"Fetch me something to eat!"

The genie returned with a silver bowl, twelve silver plates containing rich meats, two silver cups, and two bottles of wine. Aladdin's mother, when she came to herself, said:

"Fetch me something to eat!"

"Whence comes this splendid feast?"

"Ask not, but eat," replied Aladdin.

So they sat at breakfast till it was dinner-time, and Aladdin told his mother about the lamp. She begged him to sell it, and have nothing to do with devils.

"No," said Aladdin, "since chance has made us aware of its virtues, we will use it and the ring likewise, which I shall always wear on my finger." When they had eaten all the genie had brought, Aladdin sold one of the silver plates, and so on till none were left. He then had recourse to the genie, who gave him another set of plates, and thus they lived for many years.

One day Aladdin heard an order from the Sultan proclaimed that everyone was to stay at home and close his shutters while the princess, his daughter, went to and from the bath. Aladdin was seized by a desire to see her face, which was very difficult, as she always went veiled. He hid himself behind the door of the bath, and peeped through a chink. The princess lifted her veil as she went in, and looked so beautiful that Aladdin fell in love with her at first sight. He went home so changed that his mother was frightened. He told her he loved the princess so deeply that he could not live without her, and meant to ask her in marriage of her father. His mother, on hearing this, burst out laughing, but Aladdin at last prevailed upon her to go before the Sultan and carry his request. She fetched a napkin and laid in it the magic fruits from the enchanted garden, which sparkled and shone like the most beautiful jewels. She took these with her to please the Sultan, and set out, trusting in the lamp. The grand-vizir and the lords of council had just gone in as she entered the hall and placed herself in front of the Sultan. He, however, took no notice of her. She went every day for a week, and stood in the same place.

When the council broke up on the sixth day the Sultan said to his vizir: "I see a certain woman in the audience-chamber every day carrying something in a napkin. Call her next time, that I may find out what she wants."

Next day, at a sign from the vizir, she went up to the foot of the throne, and remained kneeling till the Sultan said to her: "Rise, good woman, and tell me what you want."

She hesitated, so the Sultan sent away all but the vizir, and bade her speak freely, promising to forgive her beforehand for anything she might say. She then told him of her son's violent love for the princess.

"I prayed him to forget her," she said, "but in vain; he threatened to do some desperate

deed if I refused to go and ask your Majesty
for the hand of the princess. Now I pray you
to forgive not me alone, but my son Aladdin."

The Sultan asked her kindly what she had
in the napkin, whereupon she unfolded the
jewels and presented them.

He was thunderstruck, and turning to the
vizir said: "What sayest thou? Ought I not to
bestow the princess on one who values her at
such a price?"

The vizir, who wanted her for his own son,
begged the Sultan to withhold her for three
months, in the course of which he hoped his
son would contrive to make him a richer
present. The Sultan granted this, and told
Aladdin's mother that, though he consented to
the marriage, she must not appear before him
again for three months.

Aladdin waited patiently for nearly three
months, but after two had elapsed his mother,
going into the city to buy oil, found every one
rejoicing, and asked what was going on.

"Do you not know," was the answer, "that
the son of the grand-vizir is to marry the Sultan's daughter to-night?"

Breathless, she ran and told Aladdin, who
was overwhelmed at first, but presently
bethought him of the lamp. He rubbed it, and
the genie appeared, saying: "What is thy will?"

Aladdin replied: "The Sultan, as thou knowest, has broken his promise to me, and the vizir's son is to have the princess. My command is that to-night you bring hither the bride and bridegroom."

"Master, I obey," said the genie.

Aladdin then went to his chamber, where, sure enough at midnight the genie transported the bed containing the vizir's son and the princess.

"Take this new-married man," he said, "and put him outside in the cold, and return at daybreak."

Whereupon the genie took the vizir's son out of bed, leaving Aladdin with the princess.

"Fear nothing," Aladdin said to her; "you are my wife, promised to me by your unjust father, and no harm shall come to you."

The princess was too frightened to speak, and passed the most miserable night of her life, while Aladdin lay down beside her and slept soundly. At the appointed hour the genie fetched in the shivering bridegroom, laid him in his place, and transported the bed back to the palace.

Presently the Sultan came to wish his daughter good-morning. The unhappy vizir's son jumped up and hid himself, while the princess would not say a word, and was very sorrowful.

The Sultan sent her mother to her, who said: "How comes it, child, that you will not speak to your father? What has happened?"

The princess sighed deeply, and at last told her mother how, during the night, the bed had been carried into some strange house, and what had passed there. Her mother did not believe her in the least, but bade her rise and consider it an idle dream.

The following night exactly the same thing happened, and next morning, on the princess's refusing to speak, the Sultan threatened to cut off her head. She then confessed all, bidding him ask the vizir's son if it were not so. The Sultan told the vizir to ask his son, who owned the truth, adding that, dearly as he loved the princess, he had rather die than go through another such fearful night, and wished to be separated from her. His wish was granted, and there was an end of feasting and rejoicing.

When the three months were over, Aladdin sent his mother to remind the Sultan of his promise. She stood in the same place as before, and the Sultan, who had forgotten Aladdin, at once remembered him, and sent for her. On seeing her poverty the Sultan felt less inclined than ever to keep his word, and asked the vizir's advice, who counselled him to set so high a value on the princess that no man living could come up to it.

The Sultan then turned to Aladdin's mother, saying: "Good woman, a Sultan must remember his promises, and I will remember mine, but your son must first send me forty basins of gold brimful of jewels, carried by forty slaves, led by as many other slaves, splendidly dressed. Tell him that I await his answer." The mother of Aladdin bowed low and went home, thinking all was lost.

She gave Aladdin the message, adding: "He may wait long enough for your answer!"

"Not so long, mother, as you think," her son replied. "I would do a great deal more than that for the princess." He summoned the genie, and in a few moments the eighty slaves arrived, and filled up the small house and garden.

Aladdin made them set out to the palace, two and two, followed by his mother. They were so richly dressed, with such splendid jewels in their girdles, that everyone crowded to see them and the basins of gold they carried on their heads.

They entered the palace, and, after kneeling before the Sultan, stood in a half-circle round the throne with their arms crossed, while

Aladdin's mother presented them to the Sultan.

He hesitated no longer, but said: "Good woman, return and tell your son that I wait for him with open arms."

She lost no time in telling Aladdin, bidding him make haste. But Aladdin first called the genie.

"I want a scented bath," he said, "a richly embroidered habit, a horse surpassing the Sultan's, and twenty slaves to attend me. Besides this, six slaves, beautifully dressed, to wait on my mother; and lastly, ten thousand pieces of gold in ten purses."

No sooner said than done. Aladdin mounted his horse and passed through the streets, the slaves strewing gold as they went. Those who had played with him in his childhood knew him not, he had grown so handsome.

When the Sultan saw him he came down from his throne, embraced him, and led him into a hall where a feast was spread, intending to marry him to the princess that very day.

But Aladdin refused, saying, "I must build a palace fit for her," and took his leave.

Once home he said to the genie: "Build me a palace of the finest marble, set with jasper, agate, and other precious stones. In the middle you shall build me a large hall with a dome, its four walls of massy gold and silver, each side having six windows, whose lattices, all except one, which is to be left unfinished, must be set with diamonds and rubies. There must be stables and horses and grooms and slaves; go and see about it!"

The palace was finished by next day, and the genie carried him there and showed him all his orders faithfully carried out, even to the laying of a velvet carpet from Aladdin's palace to the Sultan's. Aladdin's mother then dressed herself carefully, and walked to the palace with her slaves, while he followed her on horseback. The Sultan sent musicians with trumpets and cymbals to meet them, so that the air resounded with music and cheers. She was taken to the princess, who saluted her and treated her with great honour. At night the princess said good-bye to her father, and set out on the carpet for Aladdin's palace, with his mother at her side, and followed by the hundred slaves. She was charmed at the sight of Aladdin, who ran to receive her.

"Princess," he said, "blame your beauty for my boldness if I have displeased you."

She told him that, having seen him, she willingly obeyed her father in this matter. After the wedding had taken place Aladdin led her into the hall, where a feast was spread, and she supped with him, after which they danced till midnight.

Next day Aladdin invited the Sultan to see the palace. On entering the hall with the four-and-twenty windows, with their rubies, diamonds, and emeralds, he cried:

"It is a world's wonder! There is only one thing that surprises me. Was it by accident that one window was left unfinished?"

"No, sir, by design," returned Aladdin. "I wished your Majesty to have the glory of finishing this palace."

The Sultan was pleased, and sent for the best jewellers in the city. He showed them the unfinished window, and bade them fit it up like the others.

"Sir," replied their spokesman, "we cannot find jewels enough."

The Sultan had his own fetched, which they soon used, but to no purpose, for in a month's time the work was not half done. Aladdin, knowing that their task was vain, bade them undo their work and carry the jewels back, and the genie finished the window at his command. The Sultan was surprised to receive his jewels again and visited Aladdin, who showed him the window finished. The Sultan embraced him, the envious vizir meanwhile hinting that it was the work of enchantment.

Aladdin had won the hearts of the people by his gentle bearing. He was made captain of the Sultan's armies, and won several battles for him, but remained modest and courteous as before, and lived thus in peace and content for several years.

But far away in Africa the magician remembered Aladdin, and by his magic arts discovered that Aladdin, instead of perishing miserably in the cave, had escaped, and had married a princess, with whom he was living in great honour and wealth. He knew that the poor tailor's son could only have accomplished this by means of the lamp, and travelled night and day till he reached the capital of China, bent on Aladdin's ruin. As he passed through the town he heard people talking everywhere about a marvellous palace.

"Forgive my ignorance," he asked, "what is this palace you speak of?"

"Have you not heard of Prince Aladdin's palace," was the reply, "the greatest wonder of the world? I will direct you if you have a mind to see it."

The magician thanked him who spoke, and having seen the palace knew that it had been raised by the genie of the lamp, and became half mad with rage. He determined to get hold of the lamp, and again plunge Aladdin into the deepest poverty.

Unluckily, Aladdin had gone a-hunting for eight days, which gave the magician plenty of time. He bought a dozen copper lamps, put them into a basket, and went to the palace, crying: "New lamps for old!" followed by a jeering crowd.

The princess, sitting in the hall of four-and-twenty windows, sent a slave to find out what the noise was about, who came back laughing, so that the princess scolded her.

"Madam," replied the slave, "who can help laughing to see an old fool offering to exchange fine new lamps for old ones?"

Another slave, hearing this, said: "There is an old one on the cornice there which he can have."

Now this was the magic lamp, which Aladdin had left there, as he could not take it out hunting with him. The princess, not knowing its value, laughingly bade the slave take it and make the exchange.

She went and said to the magician: "Give me a new lamp for this."

He snatched it and bade the slave take her choice, amid the jeers of the crowd. Little he cared, but left off crying his lamps, and went out of the city gates to a lonely place, where he remained till nightfall, when he pulled out the lamp and rubbed it. The genie appeared, and at the magician's command carried him, together with the palace and the princess in it, to a lonely place in Africa.

Next morning the Sultan looked out of the window towards Aladdin's palace and rubbed his eyes, for it was gone. He sent for the vizir, and asked what had become of the palace. The vizir looked out too, and was lost in astonishment. He again put it down to enchantment, and this time the Sultan believed him, and sent thirty men on horseback to fetch Aladdin in chains. They met him riding home, bound him, and forced him to go with them on foot. The people, however, who loved him, followed, armed, to see that he came to no harm. He was carried before the Sultan, who ordered the executioner to cut off his head. The executioner made Aladdin kneel down, bandaged his eyes, and raised his scimitar to strike. At that instant the vizir, who saw that the crowd had forced their way into the courtyard and were scaling the walls to rescue Aladdin, called to the executioner to stay his hand. The people, indeed, looked so threatening that the Sultan gave way and ordered Aladdin to be unbound, and pardoned him in the sight of the crowd.

Aladdin now begged to know what he had done.

"False wretch!" said the Sultan, "come hither," and showed him from the window the place where his palace had stood.

Aladdin was so amazed that he could not say a word.

"Where is my palace and my daughter?" demanded the Sultan. "For the first I am not so deeply concerned, but my daughter I must have, and you must find her or lose your head."

Aladdin begged for forty days in which to find her, promising if he failed to return and suffer death at the Sultan's pleasure. His prayer was granted, and he went forth sadly from the Sultan's presence. For three days he wandered about like a madman, asking everyone what had become of his palace, but they only laughed and pitied him. He came to the banks of a river, and knelt down to say his prayers before throwing himself in. In so doing he rubbed the magic ring he still wore.

The genie he had seen in the cave appeared, and asked his will.

"Save my life, genie," said Aladdin, "and bring my palace back."

"That is not in my power," said the genie; "I am only the slave of the ring; you must ask the slave of the lamp."

"Even so," said Aladdin, "but thou canst take me to the palace, and set me down under my dear wife's window." He at once found himself in Africa, under the window of the princess, and fell asleep out of sheer weariness.

He was awakened by the singing of the birds, and his heart was lighter. He saw plainly that all his misfortunes were owing to the loss of the lamp, and vainly wondered who had robbed him of it.

That morning the princess rose earlier than she had done since she had been carried into Africa by the magician, whose company she was forced to endure once a day. She, however, treated him so harshly that he dared not live there altogether. As she was dressing, one of her women looked out and saw Aladdin. The princess ran and opened the window, and at the noise she made Aladdin looked up. She called to him to come to her, and great was the joy of these lovers at seeing each other again.

After he had kissed her Aladdin said: "I beg of you, Princess, in God's name, before we speak of anything else, for your own sake and mine, tell me what has become of an old lamp I left on the cornice in the hall of four-and-twenty windows, when I went a-hunting."

"Alas!" she said, "I am the innocent cause of our sorrows," and told him of the exchange of the lamp.

"Now I know," cried Aladdin, "that we have to thank the African magician for this! Where is the lamp?"

"He carries it about with him," said the princess, "I know, for he pulled it out of his breast to show me. He wishes me to break my faith with you and marry him, saying that you were beheaded by my father's command. He is for ever speaking ill of you, but I only reply by my tears. If I persist, I doubt not but he will use violence."

Aladdin comforted her, and left her for a while. He changed clothes with the first person he met in the town, and having bought a certain powder returned to the princess, who let him in by a little side door.

"Put on your most beautiful dress," he said to her, "and receive the magician with smiles, leading him to believe that you have forgotten me. Invite him to sup with you, and say you wish to taste the wine of his country. He will go for some, and while he is gone I will tell you what to do."

She listened carefully to Aladdin, and when he left her arrayed herself gaily for the first time since she left China. She put on a girdle and head-dress of diamonds, and seeing in a glass that she looked more beautiful than ever, received the magician, saying to his great amazement: "I have made up my mind that Aladdin is dead, and that all my tears will not bring him back to me, so I am resolved to mourn no more, and have therefore invited you to sup with me; but I am tired of the wines of China, and would fain taste those of Africa."

The magician flew to his cellar, and the princess put the powder Aladdin had given her in her cup. When he returned she asked him to drink her health in the wine of Africa, handing him her cup in exchange for his as a sign she was reconciled to him.

Before drinking the magician made her a speech in praise of her beauty, but the princess cut him short, saying:

"Let me drink first, and you shall say what you will afterwards." She set her cup to her lips and kept it there, while the magician drained his to the dregs and fell back lifeless.

The princess then opened the door to Aladdin, and flung her arms round his neck; but Aladdin put her away, bidding her to leave

him, as he had more to do. He then went to
the dead magician, took the lamp out of his
vest, and bade the genie carry the palace and
all in it back to China. This was done, and the
princess in her chamber only felt two little
shocks, and little thought she was at home
again.

The Sultan, who was sitting in his closet,
mourning for his lost daughter, happened to
look up, and rubbed his eyes, for there stood
the palace as before! He hastened thither, and
Aladdin received him in the hall of the four-
and-twenty windows, with the princess at his
side. Aladdin told him what had happened,
and showed him the dead body of the magician, that he might believe. A ten days' feast
was proclaimed, and it seemed as if Aladdin
might now live the rest of his life in peace; but
it was not to be.

The African magician had a younger
brother, who was, if possible, more wicked
and more cunning than himself. He travelled
to China to avenge his brother's death, and
went to visit a pious woman called Fatima,
thinking she might be of use to him. He
entered her cell and clapped a dagger to her
breast, telling her to rise and do his bidding
on pain of death. He changed clothes with her,
coloured his face like hers, put on her veil and

murdered her, that she might tell no tales. Then he went towards the palace of Aladdin, and all the people thinking he was the holy woman, gathered round him, kissing his hands and begging his blessing. When he got to the palace there was such a noise going on round him that the princess bade her slave look out of the window and ask what was the matter. The slave said it was the holy woman, curing people by her touch of their ailments, whereupon the princess, who had long desired to see Fatima, sent for her. On coming to the princess the magician offered up a prayer for her health and prosperity. When he had done the princess made him sit by her, and begged him to stay with her always. The false Fatima, who wished for nothing better, consented, but kept his veil down for fear of discovery. The princess showed him the hall, and asked him what he thought of it.

"It is truly beautiful," said the false Fatima. "In my mind it wants but one thing."

"And what is that?" said the princess.

"If only a roc's egg," replied he, "were hung up from the middle o' this dome, it would be the wonder of the world."

After this the princess could think of nothing but a roc's egg, and when Aladdin returned from hunting he found her in a very ill humour. He begged to know what was amiss, and she told him that all her pleasure in the hall was spoilt for the want of a roc's egg hanging from the dome.

"If that is all," replied Aladdin, "you shall soon be happy."

He left her and rubbed the lamp, and when the genie appeared commanded him to bring a roc's egg. The genie gave such a loud and terrible shriek that the hall shook.

"Wretch!" he cried, "is it not enough that I have done everything for you, but you must command me to bring my master and hang him up in the midst of this dome? You and your wife and your palace deserve to be burnt to ashes; but this request does not come from you, but from the brother of the African magician whom you destroyed. He is now in your palace disguised as the holy woman—whom he murdered. He it was who put that wish into your wife's head. Take care of yourself, for he means to kill you." So saying the genie disappeared.

Aladdin went back to the princess, saying his head ached, and requesting that the holy Fatima should be fetched to lay her hands on it. But when the magician came near, Aladdin, seizing his dagger, pierced him to the heart.

"What have you done?" cried the princess. "You have killed the holy woman!"

"Not so," replied Aladdin, "but a wicked

magician," and told her of how she had been deceived.

After this Aladdin and his wife lived in peace. He succeeded the Sultan when he died, and reigned for many years, leaving behind him a long line of kings.

Abou Hassan, or,
The Sleeper Awakened

IN THE CITY of Baghdad there once lived a
young man named Abou Hassan, who, having been very badly treated by his friends,
made up his mind to have nothing more to do
with them. But, as he was still very fond of
company, he used to go every evening to the
city gates, and invite the first stranger who
entered to have supper and spend the night
with him.

One evening, as he sat as usual at the gates,
a respectable-looking merchant entered, followed by a great slave; and Abou Hassan
at once stepped forward, and invited the
stranger to have supper and spend the night
with him.

Now, this stranger was not really a merchant, but the ruler of that country, the great
Caliph, Haroun Alraschid, in disguise; however, being pleased with the look of Abou
Hassan, he readily accepted his invitation.

Abou Hassan, having no idea who the stranger really was, led the way to his house, and asked his mother to send up a good supper.

The Caliph was delighted with the pleasant manners and amusing talk of Abou Hassan; and presently asked him if he was contented with his life. Abou Hassan said he was quite happy, the only thing that ever troubled him being the unjust conduct of the head priest of a mosque close by, who, with four old men who were his friends, behaved very badly to the poor people round about; and he added that he longed to be caliph for just one day, so that he might order those five tiresome persons to be well punished.

Now, the Caliph loved a good joke; so, suddenly thinking out a merry plan, he offered his host a cup of wine, into which he had secretly put a sleeping-powder. Abou Hassan, who had not noticed what his guest had done, took the wine and drank it off, and at once fell into a deep sleep.

The Caliph now told his slave to take the sleeping man upon his back and follow him to the palace, where he ordered Abou Hassan to be undressed, and placed in his own royal bed. He then told the lords and ladies of the Court to treat the stranger exactly as though he were the real caliph; and early next morning he hid behind the curtains of the room to enjoy the fun.

When Abou Hassan awoke, he was astonished to find himself in a most magnificent sleeping chamber, with a royal robe and caliph's turban lying close beside him.

As soon as he opened his eyes a concert of sweet music began; and presently Mesrour, the chief attendant, came forward and said: "Commander of the Faithful, it is time for Your Majesty to arise."

Full of amazement, Abou Hassan said: "Why do you call me by that royal title? You make a great mistake, for I am only plain Abou Hassan."

Mesrour, however, declared that he made no mistake; and then Abou Hassan, more surprised than ever, turned to a little slave boy standing near, and said: "Tell me who I am, little servant."

"Your Majesty is the great Caliph, Haroun Alraschid!" answered the little slave solemnly.

"You don't tell the truth," said Abou Hassan. Then, holding out his hand to one of the pretty ladies close by, he said: "Bite the end of my finger, fair lady, that I may know whether I am asleep or awake."

The lady bit his finger so hard that he

He was astonished to find himself in a most
magnificent sleeping chamber.

hastily snatched it away. "I am certainly awake!" he cried; "and, since you all say so, I suppose I must be the Caliph, though I'm sure I was only Abou Hassan yesterday."

The attendants now came forward and dressed the young man in the dazzling royal robes set out for him; and when he was ready, they led him into the throne-room, where he was received with shouts of welcome by the bowing lords and viziers gathered there. He ordered the usual affairs of state for the day to go forward; and conducted himself in such a princely style that the real Caliph, still secretly watching him, was delighted.

Remembering his wish of the night before, Abou Hassan presently told Giafar, the Grand Vizir, to send soldiers to seize the priest and the four old men of the mosque of whom he had spoken to his guest; and gave orders that they should be well caned, and then led through the city, mounted on asses with their faces to the tails, a crier going before them shouting: "This is the punishment of those who interfere with other people's business!"

This command was carried out; and when the sham caliph had sent a bag of gold to his mother, the state business of the day came to an end.

Abou Hassan was now led away to feast

and enjoy himself, and was taken from hall to hall, in which the various parts of a splendid feast were set out. There many beautiful ladies were waiting to amuse him; and he talked so merrily and wittily to them that the hidden Caliph could scarcely keep from laughing aloud.

At last the day came to an end; and Abou Hassan, quite tired out, leant back on a couch and fell fast asleep. The Caliph now came forward, and ordered the attendants to dress him in his own clothes again. When this was done, a slave carried the sleeping man back to his own house; and the Caliph, having had a good laugh, went to bed well satisfied with his joke.

When Abou Hassan awoke next day, he called out at once for the pretty ladies who had amused him so well the night before; and when his mother entered the room he declared that he did not know her. She was much upset on hearing this, and said: "What is wrong with you, my son?"

"I am not your son," said Abou Hassan scornfully; "I am the Caliph, Haroun Alraschid!"

His mother only laughed at this; but Abou Hassan declared all the more that he was the Caliph, and the two began to squabble so loudly that the neighbors came running in. On hearing the cause of the quarrel, they decided that Abou Hassan was quite mad; and, dragging him away from his mother, they locked him up in a madhouse.

Here he was treated very harshly, and at last began to think he had made a mistake after all. So, when his mother next came to see him, he said he now knew himself to be indeed her son; and, delighted to find that he was mad no longer, she took him home with her.

After a while, Abou Hassan began to live his old life once more; and on the very first evening he went to the city gates, to invite a stranger to be his guest, it happened that the Caliph again came past that way, in disguise.

The Caliph went up to him at once; but Abou Hassan would have nothing to do with him, saying he was the cause of his misfortunes, since he must have cast enchantment over him when last they met. He then told the pretended merchant of all that had happened to him; and the Caliph, truly sorry that his joke had brought such trouble upon the young man, quickly thought out a plan by means of which he could make up to him for what he had suffered. He told Abou Hassan that he had used no enchantments; and said that if he might only sup once more with him, all should be well next day. So Abou Hassan led the way to his house, where they spent another pleasant evening.

When supper was over, the Caliph managed again to put a sleeping-powder into his host's wine. The young man soon fell asleep; and the Caliph then ordered his slave to carry him to the palace at once.

There Abou Hassan was dressed in royal robes, as before, and placed on the couch on which he had fallen asleep at the end of his first day in the palace; and the Caliph again gave orders for him to be treated as king when he awoke.

Next morning, when Abou Hassan opened his eyes and found himself once more in the splendid hall of the palace, he was utterly astonished; and when the attendants came forward, calling him "Commander of the Faithful," he thought he must be dreaming.

But at that moment bands of music began to play, and all the lords and ladies started to sing, skip, and dance.

Abou Hassan, finding that he was certainly awake, and in some wonderful way a king once again, was so delighted that he began to join in the fun; and, tearing off his royal turban, he seized hold of the ladies' hands, and danced, sang, and cut such funny capers that the real Caliph laughed so much that he could scarcely speak.

But when the latter found his voice, he came from his hiding-place, and called out: "Abou Hassan! Abou Hassan! Do you want to kill me with laughing?"

The music stopped suddenly; and Abou Hassan, turning to where the voice came from, saw the Caliph, whom he knew by sight, and now recognized in him the merchant whom he had twice invited to supper.

He at once bowed to the ground, understanding the trick that had been played upon him; but the Caliph declared that he now meant to make amends for the sufferings his little joke had caused him. He ordered a handsome robe to be given to the young man, and said that he should live in the palace as one of his chief lords; and, later, he allowed him to marry one of the most beautiful ladies of the Court, and gave him a large sum of money with which to live in splendid style.

So Abou Hassan was made very happy indeed; and as he was never at a loss for a merry jest, he quickly became the chief favorite of the great Caliph.

Ali Baba and the Forty Thieves

ONCE UPON A TIME there were two brothers, named Ali Baba and Cassim, who lived in a certain town of Persia. These two brothers were not alike in any way, for Cassim was rich and haughty, while Ali Baba was a very poor and humble wood-cutter.

One day Ali Baba took his three asses and went into a forest as usual to cut wood. He had just finished loading his asses when he saw a number of horsemen galloping towards him; and feeling sure that they were robbers, he climbed up into a tree near a steep rock.

As the horsemen drew near, Ali Baba counted forty of them; and from the great bags of plunder that they carried, he knew they were indeed robbers. To his alarm, they stopped beneath his tree, and their leader then went forward to the rock, and called out, "Open, Sesame."

Instantly a door opened in the rock; the

robbers, with their bags, marched through, and the door shut.

Presently all the thieves trooped out again, with empty bags this time, and mounted their horses. When the last had come out, the captain said, "Shut, Sesame!" and the rock-door closed again. The robbers then rode off.

After waiting till they were out of sight, Ali Baba came down from his tree. And being curious to know what lay on the other side of the magic door, he went up to the rock and called out, "Open, Sesame!" Instantly the door flew open, and as he entered, it shut again.

Ali Baba found himself in a large, well-lighted cave, full of wonderful treasures— silks and rich cloths, and great heaps of gold, silver and jewels.

He quickly gathered together as many bags of gold as he thought his asses could carry; and having opened the door by means of the magic word, he loaded the animals with them, and set off home.

When he got to his poor hut, he emptied the bags of their precious gold; and he and his wife rejoiced together, knowing that they were now rich for life.

Greedy Cassim soon got to know of his brother's treasure, and being very jealous, he went to Ali Baba and forced him to say how he had come by so much gold.

Ali Baba found himself in a large, well-lighted
cave, full of wonderful treasures.

Having learned where the robbers' cave was, Cassim made up his mind to go there himself for treasure, not being content with the riches he already had. So next day he took ten mules into the forest, and having found the rock of which Ali Baba had told him, he stood before it and said, "Open, Sesame!" At once the door flew open, and as Cassim entered the cave, it shut of its own accord.

Quickly he gathered together a great many bags of gold and jewels; but when he was ready to come out, he found that he had forgotten the magic word that would open the door. He called out every name he could think of, but still the door remained shut.

Soon the robbers returned to the cave; and although Cassim tried to hide behind the bags of gold, they found him out, and killed him. Then they cut his body into four pieces, and hung them up on either side of the cave door, to frighten anyone else who should venture in; and having emptied their bags, they rode away once more.

Now, when Cassim did not return in the evening, his wife grew uneasy, and went to tell her fears to Ali Baba. He promised to look for her husband the next day, and early in the morning went off to the robbers' cave. The first sight that met his eyes on entering the cave was his brother's quartered body. Full of horror, he took the quarters down, and placed them on one of his asses; then, loading the two others with gold, he returned home.

He gave the dead body into the charge of a beautiful and clever slave-girl of Cassim's, called Morgiana, and she went to an old cobbler, named Baba Mustapha, who, for some pieces of gold, allowed himself to be blindfolded and led to Cassim's house. There Morgiana bade him sew up the four quarters of Cassim's body: and when this was done she blindfolded him again, and led him back to his shop. Cassim's body was then buried in the usual manner, without anyone learning the secret of his death.

A short time after, Cassim's wife was married to Ali Baba, who, taking his own family and belongings with him, went to live in his brother's house. As such marriages were common in his country, no one was surprised.

In the meantime, when the robbers came back to their cave and found Cassim's body gone, they knew that the secret of their hiding-place was known to someone else; and they made up their minds to find out all they could about the man they had killed and his friends.

So one of their number was disguised, and

sent into the town early one morning to learn
the news of the place; and the first person he
spoke to happened to be old Mustapha. It was
not long before the old cobbler told him of
the strange piece of work he had done lately;
and the robber, feeling sure that the body
Mustapha spoke of must be the one from the
cave, promised him gold if he would show
him the house he had been taken to, saying
that if he were blindfolded again he might
remember the turnings.

Mustapha agreed, and, after being blindfolded, led the way to Ali Baba's house. Then
the robber, having put a chalk-mark on the
door so he might know it again, gave the old
man his gold, and returned to the cave.

It was not long before Morgiana came out
of the house, and saw the chalk-mark on the
door. Thinking it might mean danger to her
master, she marked all the other doors in the
street with chalk, in the same way. So when
the robbers came into the street next day,
meaning to attack their enemy, they could not
tell which was the right house, and were
obliged to return to their cave.

They soon sent another of their band to find
out the house for them, and this man marked
the door with red chalk. Morgiana, however,
spied his mark also, and marked all the other

doors with red chalk, in the same manner. So when the robbers came a second time, they were no better off than before.

At last the robber captain got old Mustapha to lead him to Ali Baba's house. He did not mark the door, but noted it very carefully, so that he could not fail to know it again. He then got a number of large leather oil-jars, put a robber into each, and slung them over mules; and having disguised himself as a merchant, he led them straight to Ali Baba's house one evening, and asked if he might pass the night there, as it was growing late.

Ali Baba granted him leave to do so, and after supper he was led to the room where he was to rest.

Now, Morgiana, having run short of oil for her lamp that night, thought she would take a little from the oil-merchant's jars in the yard.

But she was filled with surprise when, on going up to one of the jars, she heard a voice whisper, "Is it time?" She was brave enough not to cry out, but to whisper in answer, "Not yet; but presently!" and, on hearing the same whisper from the other jars, to give the same answer.

She now knew that her master was in great danger, and quickly thought out a clever plan to save him. She found that one jar was really full of oil; so, filling her largest kettle from this, she put it on the fire to boil. When it was ready, she took the kettle into the yard, and poured enough of the boiling oil into each of the jars to kill instantly the man inside.

Presently she saw the robber captain creep down into the yard to call his men. But when he looked into the jars and saw that they were dead, he knew that his plot had been found out, and quickly made his escape.

Next day Morgiana told her master of all that had happened; and Ali Baba was so grateful that he said she should be a slave no longer. But Morgiana loved her master so well that she still stayed in his house.

It was not long before the robber captain thought out another plan for getting rid of his enemy. He set up as a merchant in the town, and soon made friends with Ali Baba's son, who was also a merchant. And he showered so many favors upon the young man that at last he was invited to Ali Baba's house.

Ali Baba prepared a grand feast, and when it was over Morgiana came in to dance before them.

Now, Morgiana at once recognized the robber captain, in spite of his disguise, and seeing that he had a dagger hidden inside his robe, she knew that he meant to kill Ali Baba.

But she quickly thought out a way to spoil his wicked plans once more.

In her last dance she held a scimitar high over her head, and went through all kinds of graceful movements with it; and just as the false guest was admiring her most, she suddenly rushed forward and plunged the weapon into his heart.

She then pointed out the robber captain beneath his disguise; and Ali Baba was so grateful to her for having saved his life a second time that he said she should be married to his son, as a reward.

So Morgiana and the young merchant were married a few days later. And as Ali Baba now had the secret of the robber's cave to himself, he and his family were rich and happy to the end of their days.

The Enchanted Horse

O NCE, ON A certain great feast-day, a King of Persia was admiring the many curious things which it was the custom to bring before the Court at such times, when a Hindu suddenly appeared with an artificial horse, so good an imitation that at first it was believed to be a live animal.

Bowing low before the King, the Hindu declared that the horse would instantly carry through the air any person who mounted it, to whatever place he might name.

The King asked for a proof of this; and the Hindu, mounting the horse, turned a peg in its neck, which caused it to rise in the air and vanish out of sight.

In a few moments it returned; and the Hindu, alighting, presented the King with a palm branch which he had plucked from a tree on a mountain many miles away.

The King now wished to have the magic horse for his own; but when he asked the

price of it, the Hindu answered: "The only
price I will take for my enchanted horse is
your daughter's hand in marriage."

On hearing this, the King's son, Prince
Firouz-Schah, begged his father not to think
of giving away the Princess to a mere Hindu
juggler. The King said he hoped to satisfy the
man with something else; and, in the meantime, he asked the Prince to try the horse himself.

Quickly the young prince mounted, and,
without waiting for the Hindu's directions,
turned the peg; the horse instantly rose into
the air, carrying him out of sight in a few
moments, to the alarm of the King, who now
fell into a rage and ordered the juggler to be
kept a prisoner till the Prince returned.

In the meantime, the enchanted horse was
rushing through the air at a great rate, and at
first the Prince enjoyed his ride; but when he
found that he could not make his steed return
to the ground, he was much alarmed. He was
just beginning to despair when he felt another
peg, behind the horse's right ear.

Quickly he turned this peg, and, to his joy,
the horse soon reached the earth. It was now
night, and the young prince had no idea where
he was. He jumped off the horse's back, and

by the light of the moon saw that he was standing on the marble balcony of a splendid palace. He walked a few steps till he came to an open door; and seeing a light through this, he entered.

He soon found himself in a great hall, where some slaves lay sleeping before an inner room. The Prince now knew that he was near the sleeping-chamber of some royal maiden; and stepping lightly over the slaves, he softly entered the room beyond, where he beheld the most beautiful princess he had ever seen. He fell in love with her at once, and touching the sleeve of her robe, he gently awoke her.

The Princess was astonished to find a handsome young stranger beside her; but when the Prince had explained how he came to be there, she received him very kindly, and ordered her ladies to attend to all his wants.

Next morning, the Princess, who was a daughter of the King of Bengal, asked the young prince to stay and spend some days with her. Prince Firouz-Schah was only too glad to do so; and the Princess at once ordered all kinds of gay amusements to be held in his honor.

Many happy weeks quickly passed away in

a pleasant manner; and the Prince of Persia and the Princess of Bengal soon grew to love each other.

So, when the Prince at last made up his mind to return to Persia, he soon persuaded the Princess to go with him.

The enchanted horse was brought out one morning; and having placed the Princess safely on its back, Prince Firouz-Schah sprang up beside her, and turned the peg.

The young prince guided the horse very carefully, and soon they arrived safely at his father's palace.

The King of Persia was delighted to see his son again, and gave orders for the Hindu to be set free. But the Hindu took a terrible revenge. He quietly mounted the enchanted horse when nobody was looking, and suddenly snatching up the Princess of Bengal, he turned the peg, and quickly vanished out of sight with her.

The Prince of Persia was full of grief when he saw his beloved Princess borne away on the enchanted horse, and at once began a long, lonely search for her.

Meanwhile, the Hindu carried his prize to a great distance; and when evening fell, he guided the enchanted horse to a wood near the chief city of Cashmere.

Soon they arrived safely at his father's palace.

Here he made the terrified princess alight, and began to treat her so badly that she cried aloud for help. Her cries were heard by the Sultan of Cashmere, who, riding up, ordered his guards to seize the Hindu and cut off his head.

When this was done, he took the Princess of Bengal to his palace; and the poor maiden soon found herself in another fix, for, on coming to see her next day, the Sultan was so charmed with her beauty that he declared he would make her his bride at once.

Now, the Princess was determined to marry no one but the Prince of Persia, so she pretended to go mad suddenly, uttering dreadful shrieks and wild words, and throwing herself about in the strangest way.

The Sultan ran away in terror, and ordered the wedding to be put off until the Princess got better. But she kept up her pretence of madness so well that though the Sultan sent for all the doctors in the country to cure her, none of them dared go near her.

One day, however, a poor dervish came to the palace, and declared that he could cure the Princess; so he was taken to her room at once.

Now, this dervish was really Prince Firouz-Schah, who had heard people talk of a certain mad princess of Bengal, and felt sure she must be his own lost Princess. And when the Princess saw that the dervish was really her own dear Prince, she fell into his arms and wept for joy.

After they had rejoiced together for a few minutes, they arranged a plan of escape.

When the pretended dervish came out of the room, he went straight to the Sultan, and said that as some of the magic from the enchanted horse must have entered into the Princess, the only way to cure her would be to set her on its back again and light fires around it, burning in the flames a certain incense which he alone possessed.

The Sultan was delighted to hear this, and gave orders that the directions of the dervish should be duly carried out.

So next morning the Princess of Bengal was placed on the magic horse; and when she was seated, fires were lighted all around her.

The pretended dervish then threw some incense into each of the fires, and ran three times around the horse, muttering strange words.

The incense caused such a dense cloud of smoke to arise that the Princess was completely hidden by it; then the Prince of Persia sprang up beside her and turned the peg, and the enchanted horse rose into the air and quickly vanished out of sight, the Sultan being left to swallow his disappointment as best he could.

The enchanted horse soon arrived safely in Persia; and there, in a very short time, Prince Firouz-Schah and the Princess of Bengal were married, and lived happily together for the rest of their lives.

Camaralzaman and Badoura

ONCE UPON A TIME there was a handsome young prince, named Camaralzaman, who refused to be married; and all arguments being in vain, his father, the King of Khaledan, at last shut him up in a lonely tower, until he should become more reasonable.

Now, it happened that in this tower there was a well, in which dwelt a fairy named Maimoune; and as soon as darkness fell, this fairy sprang to the mouth of the well, to wander about. She made her way to the room where Prince Camaralzaman lay sleeping; and when she saw him she stood admiring his beauty, until presently she was joined by a genie, named Danhasch.

These two were not very good friends, and a dispute soon arose between them. Maimoune said that Camaralzaman was the most beautiful person in the world; but Danhasch declared that the Princess Badoura of China, whom he had just seen, was far lovelier than the young prince. He added that this princess had displeased her father greatly by refusing to be married.

The fairy said she could not believe that the princess was more beautiful than the prince; and she ordered Danhasch to fetch the maiden, in order that they might compare the two.

So the genie flew away, and soon returned with the princess, sleeping. Even now neither he nor the fairy could agree as to which had the more beauty—the prince or the princess; so they decided to wake them each in turn, and whichever should admire the other more should be considered the less beautiful.

Prince Camaralzaman was awakened first; and he was so delighted with the dazzling beauty of the maiden beside him that he fell in love with her at once. Finding that he could not arouse her, he gave her a kiss; and then he fell asleep once more. The princess was next awakened, and when she saw the handsome young prince beside her, she also fell in love directly; but failing to wake him with her words of love and admiration, she kissed him, and then lay back again in the sleep of enchantment.

The Fairy Maimoune now declared that

Prince Camaralzaman fell in love with her at once.

Prince Camaralzaman must be considered the more beautiful, since the Princess Badoura had uttered more words of admiration for him than he had for her; and then she ordered the genie to carry the princess back to her own home.

Next morning, when Prince Camaralzaman awoke, he wished to know what had become of the beautiful lady he had seen the night before; and when his slaves declared that no one had entered his room, he flew into such a rage that they ran in terror to the palace. The king tried to comfort his son, but Camaralzaman soon fell so ill with grief for the loss of the beautiful lady he had fallen in love with, that he seemed likely to die.

Meanwhile the Princess of China was going through just another such unhappy time. On awaking the morning after her strange visit to Prince Camaralzaman, she asked her old women what they had done with the handsome young prince she had seen the night before; and when they said that no one had entered the room she acted so wildly that they fetched her father, in alarm.

When she still declared that the adventure was real, the king decided that she had gone mad, and ordered her to be shut up more closely than before, with only her old nurse to attend her. He also proclaimed that if anyone could cure his daughter, he should marry her.

Now, it happened that the princess's old nurse had a clever son, named Narzavan, who had travelled in many lands; and this youth, shocked to hear of the sad state of the poor princess, who was now really ill with grief, offered to travel through every country until he found the young man whom she loved so well.

The princess was overjoyed to hear this; so Marzavan set out the very next day. He journeyed from city to city, and from country to country, and at last came to an island where all the talk was about the strange illness and fancies of a certain Prince Camaralzaman. Marzavan decided that this must be the very person for whom he was searching, and made up his mind to visit him at once.

He soon arrived at the capital, and went to the palace; and, on saying he believed he could cure the young prince of his illness, was taken to his room, and left alone with him. When he had told the prince the whole story of the Princess Badoura, Camaralzaman sprang up and declared that this was certainly the princess with whom he had fallen in love.

He now felt quite well again; and the King of Khaledan was so delighted that he loaded Marzavan with gifts and honors.

One day the prince begged Marzavan to take him secretly to China, as he could no longer live without the beautiful Princess Badoura. Marzavan gladly agreed and they set off at once.

After a long journey and many adventures, they reached the capital of China; and having dressed himself in an astrologer's robe, Camaralzaman went straight to the royal palace, and said he had come to cure the Princess Badoura. He was taken to her room, and she, knowing at once that this was the handsome young man of her midnight adventure, ran into his arms with joy.

The king was so pleased to find his daughter well again that he gladly consented to their marriage, which took place next day amidst great rejoicings.

After several happy weeks had passed away, Camaralzaman made up his mind to return to Khaledan with his bride; and one day they set off, with a large number of soldiers and attendants. That same evening they pitched their tents beneath some shady tree; and feeling very tired, the princess fell fast asleep on a couch in one of the tents. Prince

Camaralzaman entered soon after; and noticing a pretty jewel lying beside the couch, he picked it up, and took it outside to look at it more closely.

It was the Princess Badoura's talisman; and just as the young prince was admiring it, a bird darted down and snatched it out of his hand. Camaralzaman ran after the bird, which swallowed the talisman, and went to roost on the top of a tree; then the prince, determined not to return without the jewel, went to sleep on the ground.

For ten days Camaralzaman followed the bird, but as they approached a strange city near the seashore, it flew over a high wall, and he lost sight of it. Then, full of despair, he entered the city, where he lived for some time.

Meanwhile the Princess Badoura had learnt of the loss of her talisman and the disappearance of her husband. At first she was full of despair; but finally she dried her tears, and made up her mind to go on with her journey. Thinking she would be safer in the disguise of a man, she dressed up in some of her husband's clothes, and traveled as Prince Camaralzaman.

Coming to the sea, she set sail on board a ship. The vessel, however, went to pieces in a terrible storm, and the princess was cast upon the shores of the Isle of Ebony. Here she was received very kindly as Prince Camaralzaman by the king; and, not daring to tell him who she really was, in a very short time she was married to the Princess of Ebony (to whom she told her whole story, and who promised to keep her secret), and was crowned King of Ebony in the old king's place.

Whilst Badoura was reigning as king in Ebony, the real Prince Camaralzaman was still living in the strange city, waiting for a vessel to sail, which happened only once a year.

One day, noticing some glittering thing hanging from the dead body of a bird, he picked it up, and found to his surprise and joy that it was the Princess Badoura's talisman. That same day he also found a great treasure of gold dust, which he placed carefully in olive jars, together with the princess's talisman; and as the yearly vessel was now ready to start, he sent his jars on board, and then went to bid farewell to the old man with whom he had lived in the city.

Seeing that he was about to die, however, Camaralzaman stayed with him till the last, and buried him. Then he found that the ship had sailed without him; and, full of grief, he went back to wait another year.

Now the ship in which he should have sailed stopped at the Isle of Ebony; and the captain decided to sell the olive jars, and to give the money he got for them to Camaralzaman on his return.

Some of these jars were bought for the pretended King of Ebony, who was very fond of olives; but when Badoura had one of them opened in her presence, she was astonished to find it full of gold dust, and her surprise was greater still when presently her talisman was found at the bottom of the jar. Learning from the captain of the ship all he knew about the owner of the jars, she ordered him to bring the young man from the strange city to her as quickly as possible.

Prince Camaralzaman was only too glad to go with the captain; and when he arrived at the Isle of Ebony, he was taken at once into the presence of the pretended king, in whom he was overjoyed to discover his long-lost princess.

When the whole strange story had been told to the old king, he decided that the real prince should now rule as king. So Camaralzaman was crowned King of Ebony, and settled down to a life of happiness and peace.

The Seven Voyages of
Sindbad the Sailor

A POOR PORTER, named Hindbad, one day, drawing near to a large house in Baghdad, from which sounds of gay music were coming, sat down on the pavement outside, to listen, and to rest himself. A grand feast was going on inside; and Hindbad soon learnt that this was the house of the famous Sindbad the Sailor.

The poor porter had often heard of the wealth of this great sailor; and now, comparing his own sad lot with the easy life of the rich man at whose gate he sat, he could not help crying out: "What has Sindbad done to deserve such happiness? And what have I done that I should be so wretched?"

Now, this complaint was heard by those within the house; and presently a slave came out to take Hindbad before his master. The poor porter was quite dazzled by the richness of the feasting-hall, and bowed humbly to the gaily-dressed guests. The great Sindbad received him very kindly, and made him sit down beside him, saying: "My friend, I heard your complaint just now, and do not blame you. Yet you make a mistake if you imagine that I reached my present happiness without much suffering and trouble. If my guests are willing, I will tell you the story of my seven voyages; and from that you will see that what I say is the truth."

The guests were ready enough to listen to the story of the great sailor's adventures, and Sindbad began the tale of his first voyage.

SINDBAD'S FIRST VOYAGE

"When my father died he left me a good fortune, which I enjoyed for some time: but a great love of adventure soon made me give up my easy life, and take to the sea. I threw in my lot with some merchants; and having fitted out a trading vessel, we set sail, calling at various islands to buy and sell goods.

"One day three of us landed on a small island; but no sooner had we made a fire to cook our food than the island began to tremble and quake most horribly. Then we saw

that what we had taken for an island was
really the back of a huge whale; and, full of
fright, we made a wild rush for our ship.
Before I could get away, however, the monster
dived in the sea, tossing me into the waves;
and by the time I rose to the surface I found
that the ship had sailed away, the captain having thought that I was drowned. I clung to a
piece of wood which I managed to seize; and
after struggling with the waves for many
hours, I was at length flung upon the shores of
an island.

"I rested for a while, and after eating some
wild fruits walked forward into the island.
Soon I came to a plain, where I found a very
handsome horse feeding; and whilst I was
admiring his beauty, a man came up, and
asked what I was doing there. I told him my
story, and then he led me to a cave, where a
number of other men were resting. They gave
me some food, and, whilst I was eating, told
me that they were grooms to the great King
Mihrage, who ruled over the island; and were
now going to his palace with the fine horse I
had seen.

"Next day they set off for the capital, taking
me with them. King Mihrage received me very
kindly, and invited me to stay with him as

long as I pleased. I saw many curious things in that island, and learnt much from the merchants and learned Indians there.

"Ships from all parts often came to the harbor; and one day, as I stood watching a merchant vessel unloading some bales, I saw, to my surprise, that these goods were marked with my own name.

"I went on board, and, finding that the captain was indeed the one with whom I had set sail, made up my mind to return with him.

"I took some of my best bales as a gift to King Mihrage; and having thanked him for his kindness, I set sail once more.

"We traded at the various islands we passed, and at last arrived safely at Balsora. I made my way at once to Baghdad with the large sum of money I had got for my bales; and building a fine house, I gave money away to the poor, and settled down to enjoy my good fortune."

Sindbad stopped his story here, and, giving a hundred sequins to Hindbad, invited him to come back next day, when he should hear more of his adventures.

Next day another feast was held; and as soon as Hindbad and the other guests had finished, Sindbad began the story of his second voyage.

SINDBAD'S SECOND VOYAGE

"I soon grew tired of an idle life, and went to sea again with another party of merchants.

"One day we landed on a desert island. After wandering about for a time I felt tired, and lay down in a quiet spot to sleep. When I awoke, I found, to my horror, that the ship had sailed without me, and that I was left alone.

"At first I was full of despair, but after a while I began to look about me. I soon noticed a huge white object lying a little distance off; and making my way up to it, I found it was as smooth as ivory. As I stood wondering what it could be, the sky suddenly grew dark; and to my surprise, I found that this darkness was caused by a monster bird flying down towards me. I had often heard sailors talk of a giant bird called the roc; and I made up my mind that this was one, and that the huge white object beside me was its egg.

"Seeing in this bird a means of escape, when she reached the ground I tied myself with my turban to one of her legs, which was as thick as the trunk of a tree; and when she flew away next morning, she carried me with her. She rose to a great height, and then came down so suddenly that I fainted.

"When I again opened my eyes, I had just time to free myself from her when the roc flew away again. I now saw that I had been left in a deep valley, entirely shut in on every side by such high, rocky mountains that it was impossible to climb them. The valley was strewn with dazzling diamonds of the largest size; and as I had nothing better to do, I filled my clothing with them.

"To my terror, at one end of the valley I saw a swarm of dreadful serpents. Finding, however, that they came out only at night, I wandered about, seeking a way of escape, until night came, when I shut myself in a cave for safety.

"Next day, I was surprised to see pieces of raw meat being thrown down into the valley; but I soon understood what this meant. A party of merchants on the rocks above, not being able to get into the valley, had found that they could obtain the diamonds by means of a clever trick. They threw pieces of raw meat down; these fell upon the sharp points of the diamonds, which stuck into them; and so, when eagles carried the meat to their nests on the tops of the rocks, they carried with it a number of diamonds. The merchants then frightened the eagles off their nests, and picked the diamonds from the meat they found there.

"When I had watched this for a little, I thought of a means of escape. I tied a large piece of raw meat on to my back by means of my turban, and lay down flat on my face. Presently one of the largest eagles caught me up by the piece of meat on my back, and flew away with me to its nest above.

"You may guess how surprised the merchants were to find me there. I told them my story, and as they were returning home next day, I went with them. After many adventures, I arrived in Baghdad; and having made a huge fortune, I gave large gifts to the poor, and began to live in splendid style."

Sindbad, having ended this story, gave Hindbad another hundred sequins, and invited him to come again next day to hear about this third voyage.

You may be sure that the porter did not forget to come; and when the guests had all feasted, Sindbad went on with his story.

SINDBAD'S THIRD VOYAGE

"It was not long before I set sail once again, with another party of merchants, to seek adventures and treasure. One day we were caught in a terrible storm, and driven into the harbor of the first island we reached. No sooner had we entered this harbor than a swarm of frightful savages came swimming towards us, and climbed into the ship; they were so fierce, and came in such numbers, that we could not keep them back. They made us go on shore and left us there, taking our ship away with them.

"We wandered about the island, seeking food; and coming to a huge palace that seemed to be empty, we entered, and found ourselves in a large hall, into which there suddenly came a dreadful black giant, who had but one eye in the middle of his forehead. He had fearful, long teeth, and nails like an eagle's claws; and was so frightful to look at, that we all fell down, and lay on the floor like dead men.

"When we opened our eyes again, the ogre suddenly seized the fattest of our number; and, thrusting a spit through him, roasted and ate him. He then lay down and fell asleep.

"Full of terror, we wandered about the island all next day, seeking some means of escape, but finding none; and when evening came the ogre appeared again, and made his supper off another of my companions.

"This went on for several days; but at last I suggested that we should try to escape by sea. We found plenty of wood about the shore for rafts; and when these were ready, we returned to the palace for the last time.

"The ogre came as usual, and, having eaten another of our party for his supper, lay down and fell asleep. Those of us who were left then seized the spits, and, making them red-hot in the fire, thrust them all at once into the giant's great eye, and blinded him. We then ran down to the shore, and jumping on to our rafts, pushed them out to sea.

"But we had not gone far when the giant appeared, with several others as large as himself, who, throwing great stones at us, sank all the rafts, except the one I was on with two companions. Having managed to get out to sea, we were at last thrown upon another island; and here we were attacked by a most fearful serpent, which swallowed both my companions. I escaped from it, however, and rushing down to the shore was overjoyed to see a ship not very far away.

"I managed to attract the notice of the captain, who sent a boat to take me to the ship; and I found, to my surprise, that he was the captain with whom I had sailed on my second voyage, when I was left on the desert island. He was delighted to see me again, and showed me my own bales of goods, still untouched.

"After trading with him for some time, I arrived safely in Baghdad once more, with riches so great that I knew not their value."

When Sindbad had finished this story, he gave Hindbad another hundred sequins and next day he began the story of his fourth voyage.

SINDBAD'S FOURTH VOYAGE

"My love of adventure soon took me on board another merchant ship. We had not been long at sea, however, when we were caught in a sudden gale; and our ship was soon dashed to pieces on a rock, I and a few others being cast ashore on a strange land.

"Here we were seized by some cannibals, who took us to their huts. I soon found out that they meant to eat us as soon as we grew fat enough; and for this reason I ate scarcely any of the food they gave us. Seeing that I kept very thin, they left me alone; and after a while I managed to escape from them.

"After wandering about for eight days, I met with some civilized people. They took me to their king, who received me very kindly, and made me live at his court. .

"One day the king told me that he wished me to marry a lady of his court. I dared not disobey his command, for fear of offending him; and so I was married at once. My wife, however, very soon died; and then I found out that it was the custom there for the living husband to be buried with the dead wife.

"After my wife, dressed in her most gorgeous robes and jewels, had been first put in, I was lowered to the bottom of a large cave, and given seven small loaves to keep me alive a little longer. The top of the cave was then covered over, and I was left to my fate. I made my loaves last as many days as I could, and when I had eaten the last morsel I prepared to die. Just then, however, I heard something panting and moving in the cave, and following this sound as best I could, I came to a passage which led out on to the seashore.

"Delighted at my escape, I returned to the cave, and gathered together as many of the rich clothes and jewels as I could find in the dark.

"Having brought my treasures out, and made them up into bales, I waited on the shore until a ship should pass. A merchant vessel soon came by; and hearing my cries, the captain took me on board. This ship was going to my own country; and so, after trading with my goods, I again arrived in Baghdad with great riches."

Sindbad stopped here, and, giving the porter another purse of a hundred sequins, invited him to come the following day to hear the story of his fifth voyage. Hindbad did not fail to come; and Sindbad went on with his story.

SINDBAD'S FIFTH VOYAGE

"In spite of all the dangers I had gone through, I very soon went off to sea again; and this time I sailed in a ship of my own, joined by some merchant friends.

"We made a long voyage; and the first place we stopped at was a desert island, where we found a roc's egg, as large as the one I had seen before. It was just ready to be hatched; and my companions, in spite of my warning, soon broke open the shell with their axes, and dragging the young roc out, roasted and ate it.

"No sooner had they finished their feast than the two parent rocs appeared in the sky, flying towards us. They seemed to be in a frightful rage when they found their young one gone; and as we rushed on board our ship, they flew after us, dropping great stones from their huge claws into the vessel, with such force that it broke into a thousand pieces. I was the only one who escaped drowning; and, after a struggle, at last reached the shores of an island not far away.

"Next day, as I walked about under the trees, I came across a wild-looking old man, who asked me to carry him over a stream.

"No sooner had I lifted him on to my back, however, than the wretched old creature suddenly clasped his legs firmly round my neck, and, sitting astride my shoulders, ordered me to carry him up and down. I was obliged to carry him in this manner all day; nor would he let me go when night came, but kept his arms tightly clasped round my neck whilst I slept.

"Next day, and for many days after, he made me carry him again, and I saw that the wicked old creature meant to kill me in time. But at last I thought out a plan of escape. I squeezed some grape-juice into an empty gourd-shell one day, and coming to it some days later, I found that it was already very good wine. I drank some of it; and seeing that it refreshed me, the old man asked for some. I gave him the shell at once, and was glad to find that the wine made him lively and careless.

"Presently, to my joy, he loosened his hold

"The wretched old creature suddenly clasped his
legs firmly round my neck."

of me, so that I was able to shake him off my back; and quickly seizing a large stone, I crushed the life out of the tiresome old wretch. I then hurried down to the beach, where I met with some sailors, who took me on board their ship; and when I told them my story, they said I had had a very narrow escape, since I had fallen into the clutches of the famous Old Man of the Sea, who never let his victims go till he had strangled them.

"We soon landed on another island; and there I did such a fine trade in cocoanuts that at last I was able to go on board a merchant ship that called at the island. Thus I arrived again in Baghdad, where I was glad to settle down to an easy life once more."

Having finished this story, Sindbad sent the porter away with another hundred sequins; and next day he began the story of his sixth voyage.

SINDBAD'S SIXTH VOYAGE

"I had been at home only a year, when I made up my mind to go to sea again. This time, I took a longer voyage than I had ever been before; and we met with such stormy weather that our ship was driven out of her way altogether, and dashed to pieces on a rocky shore.

"The cliffs there rose up into a steep mountain, impossible to climb; and the fearful current that had brought us would have kept us from sailing away, even if we had had a boat. So we divided the food we had saved equally amongst us; and I spent my time wandering about, and found many rich goods and treasures that had been cast ashore from wrecks, and in one place saw a strange river which flowed swiftly into a cave.

"My companions died off, one by one, until at last I was left alone; and then I made up my mind to try to escape by means of the strange underground river, which I felt must surely have an outlet on the other side of the mountain. I soon made a strong raft; and then, having loaded it with the treasures I had found, I guided it into the cave, and for days floated in utter darkness, soon falling into a half-fainting state.

"When I once more opened my eyes, I found myself lying in a meadow, with a number of natives standing about me. I went with them to the capital of Serendib, as that island was called; and there they presented me to their king, who received me with great honor.

"After spending some happy months there, I

asked to be allowed to return to my own land; and the king ordered a ship to be got ready for me, and gave me many fine gifts, also sending a letter and a handsome present to my sovereign lord, the Caliph Haroun Alraschid.

"When I arrived at Baghdad, I presented the King's letter and gift to the Caliph, who was delighted to receive them, and sent me away with a handsome present."

Sindbad stopped here, and gave the porter his usual hundred sequins; and next day he began the story of his seventh and last voyage.

SINDBAD'S LAST VOYAGE

"As I was now growing old, I made up my mind to go to sea no more; but one day the Caliph sent for me, and begged me so hard to take a return letter and gift from him to the King of Serendib that I could not well refuse. And so I set sail once again.

"I arrived safely in Serendib; and having presented the Caliph's letter and gift to the King, I set sail homewards. We had not been at sea long, however, when our ship was seized by fierce pirates, who afterwards sold us as slaves when we landed in a strange country.

"I was bought by a rich merchant, who treated me kindly. Finding that I could shoot well with bow and arrow, he took me to a forest, and told me to shoot elephants for him. I climbed into a tall tree, and shot at the great animals as they tramped beneath; and every day I managed to kill an elephant for my master.

"But one day, to my dismay, one of the largest elephants rooted up the tree on which I was sitting, and then, followed by the rest of the herd, carried me to what was evidently their burying-place, for the ground was covered with bones and tusks; and I made up my mind that the elephants had brought me there to show me that I could get as much ivory as I wanted without killing any more of them.

"I told my master of the great treasure of ivory, and he was so delighted that he said I should be a slave no longer; and he ordered a ship to be got ready to take me back to my own land, loading it with ivory tusks for me.

"I traded with my ivory at various places; and when I once more arrived safely in Baghdad, I brought more riches than I had ever owned before.

"Having told the Caliph the story of my

adventures, I returned home, to settle down and enjoy my vast riches in peace and comfort."

When Sindbad had finished his story, he said to Hindbad: "You have now heard, my friend, of the many dangers and sufferings I have gone through. Do you not think I deserve to spend the rest of my life in ease and enjoyment?"

"Ah, yes, my lord!" answered the porter, humbly kissing Sindbad's hand. "My own poor troubles are as nothing; and I hope you may long live to enjoy the riches you have gained at such a cost."

Sindbad was so pleased with this reply that, giving Hindbad yet another hundred sequins, he begged him to give up his work as a porter and come to feast with him every day.

So Hindbad became a rich and happy man, and all the rest of his life had good cause to remember the kindness of Sindbad the Sailor.